The Grumpy Bunny Goes West

by Justine Korman

illustrated by Lucinda McQueen

Troll

For the cast and crew of
"A Bad Day at Gopher's Breath"
—J.K.

For Janine and Kristin, my favorite cowbunnies
Love, Lucy

Text copyright © 1997 by Justine Korman.
Illustrations copyright © 1997 by Lucinda McQueen.

Published by WhistleStop, an imprint
and registered trademark of Troll Communications L.L.C.

Grumpy Bunny is a trademark of Justine Korman, Lucinda McQueen,
and Troll Communications L.L.C.

Printed in the United States of America.
ISBN 0-8167-4298-7

10   9   8   7   6   5   4

At the end of the busy Easter season, Sir Byron gathered all the Easter bunnies together at the Eggworks Factory. "Once again, it is time to announce the Employee of the Year," said the Great Hare. "All of you have worked very hard. But one bunny has gone above and beyond . . ."

Hopper the grumpy bunny sighed. Speeches were *so* boring.

Then he heard something that made his ears stand straight up.

"And the winner is—Hopper!" said Sir Byron.

"Me?" Hopper squeaked happily.

"Yes, you, Hopper," Sir Byron said with a smile. "And this year's prize is a two-week vacation at Slim's Dude Ranch out West."

Hopper's ears drooped. *A dude ranch!* he thought. *Why would anyone want to go to a dusty old dude ranch?* After long hours painting Easter eggs and puffing marshmallow chicks, the only thing Hopper wanted to do was rest and relax.

But when he tried to tell Sir Byron he didn't want to go, the Great Hare just said, "No need to thank me, my boy. Enjoy yourself!"

And in no time at all, Hopper found himself out West and face-to-face with one of the biggest bunnies he'd ever seen. The bunny shook Hopper's paw hard enough to hurt, then said in a loud, jolly voice, "Howdy, stranger! I'm Slim."

"Let me show you where you'll be bedding down," Slim offered. After his long, dusty trip, Hopper wanted to sink into a big, soft bed—and not wake up until this silly vacation was over.

"You'll sleep here in the bunkhouse for the first week," Slim said. "Then we'll hit the trail."

The other guests chatted excitedly as they unpacked.
Hopper looked around the bunkhouse. No big, soft bed.
No TV. The grumpy bunny sighed. *This is going to be a very long two weeks*, he thought sadly.

Slim gave each guest a pair of real cowbunny boots, a hat, and a pair of chaps. He told them, "While you're at the ranch, you'll help out with the chores."

Hopper frowned. Who ever heard of doing chores on vacation?

Once they were all in their cowbunny gear, Slim gave each guest a horse to ride. "Why don't you take Ol' Paint?" Slim said to Hopper. "He's a nice gentle horse."

Hopper took the reins. Ol' Paint looked just as bored as the grumpy bunny himself.

But he perked up the minute Hopper climbed into the saddle! Everyone laughed when the "gentle" horse threw Hopper all over the corral.

Each time the grumpy bunny landed on the ground, Slim said, "Get back up! Remember, a cowbunny never quits."
I'm no cowbunny, Hopper thought crankily.

And sure enough, Hopper wasn't any better at shooting with a bow and arrow, learning to do rope tricks, or square dancing.

This is the dumbest vacation ever, the grumpy bunny
thought grumpily.

Things got even worse. While everyone else learned how to rope a calf, Hopper only managed to snag his own feet.

"I quit!" the grumpy bunny muttered.

But Slim just shook his head. "A cowbunny never quits." He unwound the rope from around Hopper's feet. "Be strong! Show that calf who's boss."

Hopper stared at the calf. He twirled his rope. He threw it and . . . *SWOOSH!* The lasso landed around the calf's neck! But before Hopper even had a chance to smile, the calf yanked him through the air.

Slim grinned. "I've never seen a cowbunny get roped before.
But don't be discouraged. We've got plenty more fun things to do."
Hopper groaned as he staggered to his feet.

By the time the day arrived to hit the trail, Hopper was completely miserable.

"OK, pardners, saddle up!" called Slim. "Let's keep this herd together and move 'em out!"

With a loud "Yee-ha!" the cowbunnies left the ranch.

Hopper soon discovered that the only thing he liked less than being at the ranch was being on the trail. Every day, the cowbunnies rode from sunup to sunset, moving the large, mooing herd.

"This is boring!" Hopper grumbled. "I'm sick of eating beans, tired of listening to stories, and I never, ever want to sing another song around a campfire!"

One morning, Slim said, "I've got a special treat for you cowbunnies! Today we're going to visit an old gold mine."

"Yee-ha!" the other guests cried happily.

But not Hopper. His tail was sore from riding.
He was *really* sick of beans. And, most important, the mine
looked scary. "It's too dark to see anything in there," the
trembling bunny objected.

Slim chuckled and handed Hopper a flashlight.

"Come along, pardner," he said. "A cowbunny never walks
away from something just because he's scared."

Hopper stepped into the dark mine.

"I want y'all to grab a pardner's paw," Slim told the group. "This here mine has more twists and turns than a porcupine has quills. Some even say it's haunted by the ghosts of miners who took a wrong turn and never found their way out."

Hopper shuddered. Suddenly, something screeched right
by his ear. *"Eeeeek!"* Hopper screamed and started to run out
of the mine.

"Wait! It was only a bat. He won't hurt you," Slim called
after him. But the grumpy bunny had seen enough of the
ghostly gold mine.

"I'll wait outside," Hopper said in a shaky voice.

Before the cowbunnies hit the trail again, Slim counted the cattle. "We're one calf short!" he exclaimed.

"Ringo's missing," one of his helpers realized.

"We've got to find that calf," Slim said. "Everybody spread out and start looking!"

Hopper wandered around, halfheartedly looking for Ringo. Soon he found himself outside the mine.

The grumpy bunny peered inside just in time to catch a glimpse of a cow's tail disappearing into the blackness.

Hopper's stomach dropped like a bucket down a deep well. He wanted to go for help, but he knew Ringo might be hopelessly lost by the time he returned.

The grumpy bunny thought hard. No one would know if he just pretended not to have seen the calf at all. But, scared as he was, Hopper couldn't leave poor Ringo all alone in that spooky mine.

Hopper took a deep breath and marched into the mine.
Eeek! Eeek! Shriek! Bats squeaked all around Hopper's
ears. He ran back to the entrance. But Slim's words wouldn't
stop echoing in Hopper's mind: *A cowbunny never walks
away from something just because he's scared.*

Hopper headed back into the darkness. He followed a low moo down a narrow passage, and there, right in front of him, was Ringo!

Hopper swung his rope. *Swoosh!* It fell over Ringo's head and slipped down around his neck.

"I did it!" Hopper shouted—just as Ringo bolted.

"Oh, no, you don't!" Hopper held the rope with all his might. "I'm the boss here," he told the calf firmly.

After that, Ringo was happy to follow Hopper back to camp. The calf was even happier to see his relieved mother.

Slim beamed with pride. "I reckon you're a true cowbunny after all, Hopper."

Hopper could hardly believe his ears. For the rest of the day, he didn't even think about his sore tail. Instead, he made up a song about being a real cowbunny:

A cowbunny may fall off his horse
and land in a gopher pit;
He might get snared in his own lasso
or be scared out of his wits.
But as long as there's sand in sandwiches,
a cowbunny must have grit.
For a cowbunny can do anything,
'cause a cowbunny never quits!

When Hopper finished singing,
all the cowbunnies cheered.

Later, Hopper snuggled into his bedroll. The grumpy bunny no longer minded sleeping under the stars twinkling in the big western sky. In fact, Hopper looked for the brightest one and whispered, "I wish this vacation would never end!"